THAT'S GOOD! THAT'S BAD!

Margery Cuyler

pictures by David Catrow

HENRY HOLT AND COMPANY
NEW YORK

For Brother Gren—
that's good!   M.C.

To Hillary and D.J.—
I love you dearly.   D.C.

Henry Holt and Company, Inc.
Publishers since 1866
115 West 18th Street
New York, New York 10011

An Owlet Book and colophon are registered
trademarks of Henry Holt and Company, Inc.

Published in Canada by Fitzhenry & Whiteside Ltd.,
195 Allstate Parkway, Markham, Ontario L3R 4T8.

Library of Congress Cataloging-in-Publication Data
Cuyler, Margery.
   That's good! That's bad / by Margery Cuyler ;
pictures by David Catrow.
   Summary: A little boy has a series of adventures and
misadventures with a bunch of wild animals.
   [1. Animals—Fiction.]   1. Catrow, David, ill.   II. Title.
PZ7.C997Th   1991
[E]—dc20   90-49353

ISBN 0-8050-1535-3 (hardcover)
10 9 8 7 6 5 4 3 2
ISBN 0-8050-2954-0 (paperback)
10 9 8 7 6 5 4 3 2 1

First published in hardcover in 1991 by Henry Holt and Company, Inc.
First Owlet paperback edition, 1993

Printed in the United States of America on acid-free paper. ∞

One day a little boy went to the zoo with his mother and father. They bought him a shiny red balloon.

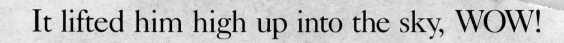

It lifted him high up into the sky, WOW!

Oh, that's good.
No, *that's bad!*

The balloon drifted for miles and miles until it came to a hot, steamy jungle. It broke on the branch of a tall, prickly tree, POP!

Oh, that's bad.
No, *that's good!*

The little boy fell into a muddy river, SPLAT!

He climbed up onto a roly-poly hippopotamus
and rode to shore, GIDDYAP!

Oh, that's good.
No, that's bad!

Ten noisy baboons were squabbling in the grass by the river. They chased the little boy up a tree until he was out of breath, PANT, PANT!

Oh, that's bad.
No, *that's good!*

The baboons wanted to play
vine-swing with the little boy,
WHAT FUN! The little boy
grabbed a vine and swung out
of their reach, WHEEEE!

Oh, that's good.
No, that's bad!

The vine was a big, scary snake that wiggled and jiggled and hissed, SSSSS!

Oh, that's bad.
No, that's good!

The little boy lost his grip, WHOOPS! and
landed on the back of a giraffe, HOORAY!

Oh, that's good.
No, that's bad!

The giraffe leaned over to drink
some swampy water, GLUG! GLUG!
The little boy slid down its neck and fell
into some quicksand next to an elephant, SLOP!

Oh, that's bad.
No, that's good!

The elephant grabbed the little boy with its trunk
and lifted him up, up, up onto its shoulders, WHOOSH!

Oh, that's good.
No, that's bad!

The elephant thumped bumpily along
to a grassy plain where it stopped
to feed. The little boy climbed down
its trunk and woke up a daddy lion
snoring in the grass, ZZZZZ!

Oh, that's bad.
No, that's good!

When the lion saw the little boy, it purred, RRRRR!
and licked the little boy's face, SLURP!

Oh, that's good.
No, that's bad!

The little boy got all wet and sticky, YUCK! and ran deeper into the jungle. It was as dark as night, OOOO! and the little boy was afraid. He sat down and started to cry, BOO-HOO!

Oh, that's bad.
No, that's good!

His tears made such a big puddle that a stork came along
to have a drink, SSSSIP! It picked up the little boy
with its beak, WHISH!

Oh, that's good.
No, that's bad!

The stork flew the little boy across the dark, windy sky,
FLAP, FLAP! The little boy thought he would never see his
parents again, SOB!

Oh, that's bad.
No, *that's good!*

The stork knew where it was going. It took the little
boy back to the zoo and dropped him into his parents' arms,
PLOP! His mother and father were so happy to see him,
they gave him a big hug and a big kiss, SMACK!

Oh, that's good.
No, that's GREAT!